First Pooch
The Obamas Pick a Pet

by **Carole Boston Weatherford**

illustrated by **Amy Bates**

Marshall Cavendish Children

Marshall Cavendish Corporation, 99 White Plains Road, Tarrytown, NY 10591
www.marshallcavendish.us/kids

Library of Congress Cataloging-in-Publication Data

Weatherford, Carole Boston, 1956-
First pooch : the Obamas pick a pet / by Carole Boston Weatherford ; Illustrated by Amy Bates. — 1st ed.
p. cm.
ISBN 978-0-7614-5636-0
1. Presidents' pets—United States—Anecdotes—Juvenile literature. 2. Obama, Barack—Family—Anecdotes—Juvenile literature. 3.
Presidents—United States—Family—Anecdotes—Juvenile literature. I. Bates, Amy June, ill. II. Title.
E176.48.W43 2009
973.932092—dc22
2009006117

The illustrations are rendered in watercolor, pencil and gouache.

Book design by Anahid Hamparian
Editor: Margery Cuyler
Printed in China
First edition
1 3 5 6 4 2

Marshall Cavendish
Children

For my Katie, her Troy, and their Sadie
—A.B.

To Hendrix, my fourth pooch and third beagle
—C.B.W.

Want a friend in Washington?
Get a dog.
—President Harry Truman

GEORGE WASHINGTON

JOHN Q. ADAMS

THOMAS JEFFERSON

ANDREW JACKSON

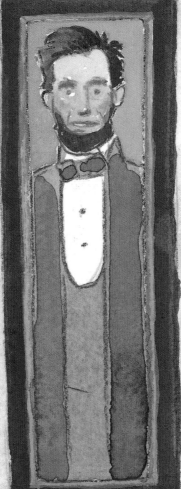

ULYSSES S. GRANT

MARTIN VAN BUREN

ABRAHAM LINCOLN

GROVER CLEVELAND

THEODORE ROOSEVELT

FRANKLIN D. ROOSEVELT

HARRY S. TRUMAN

DWIGHT D. EISENHOWER

JOHN F. KENNEDY

RICHARD M. NIXON

RONALD REAGAN

WILLIAM J. CLINTON

BARACK OBAMA

Presidents make plenty of promises.

Calvin Coolidge promised to put a chicken in every pot and a car in every garage.

John F. Kennedy promised
that we would land a man
on the moon.

And when Barack Obama threw his hat in the ring to become the forty-fourth president, he promised his daughters a puppy.

Heaven knows, Malia and Sasha had been begging to get a dog for months. Throughout the twenty-two-month-long campaign, they never once stopped wishing for a dog. They wore curls and party dresses to join their parents onstage before crowds of thousands. They put up with Secret Service agents always on their heels.

They obeyed their grandmother while Mommy and Daddy were on the campaign trail. They followed their parents' busy travel schedule, even though that made their heads spin. They figured it was worth it if they finally got their dog.

When the votes were counted on election night, the sisters felt as if they had won too. "Malia and Sasha will get their new puppy," said their dad in his victory speech.

Now the whole family had decisions to make. Daddy had to choose people to work with him in the White House. Mommy had to choose a new school for the girls.

Malia and Sasha had to decorate their new bedrooms. And
they had to choose their dog.

PRESIDENT GEORGE WASHINGTON WITH ONE OF HIS FOXHOUNDS

That would not be easy. The whole nation tried to guess which breed would wind up in the Oval Office. Would the First Daughters choose a foxhound like President George Washington's or a chocolate Labrador retriever like President Bill Clinton's?

PRESIDENT BILL CLINTON WITH "BUDDY"

Or would the girls take the lead from presidents Franklin D. Roosevelt and George W. Bush and settle on a Scottish terrier?

What if Malia and Sasha chose a foreign breed? An English
bulldog, a Peruvian hairless, or a German shepherd?
Would the American people think them unpatriotic?

After all, the First Dog had important duties.

Meeting the presidential helicopter.

Fetching the
presidential
slippers.

Negotiating treats.

Greeting heads of state.

And guarding the Rose Garden against invasion. No time for catnaps in the Lincoln Bedroom.

Sasha and Malia's parents preferred a shelter dog. "A lot of shelter dogs are mutts like me," the president-elect told the press.

Strays across the country perked up their ears.
Resumes poured in from First Pooch wannabes.

But Malia had an allergy. That ruled out some breeds: collie, komondor, and Lhasa apso, to name a few.

For weeks the family looked into breeds that would not trigger sneezes—from French poodles to labradoodles. But the president nixed a "yappy" or "girly" dog.

The family finally settled on the Portuguese water dog. Then talk turned to a name. Frank? Moose? "All bad," said the First Lady. The press hounded the president about when the pet would arrive. "That's top secret," he said.

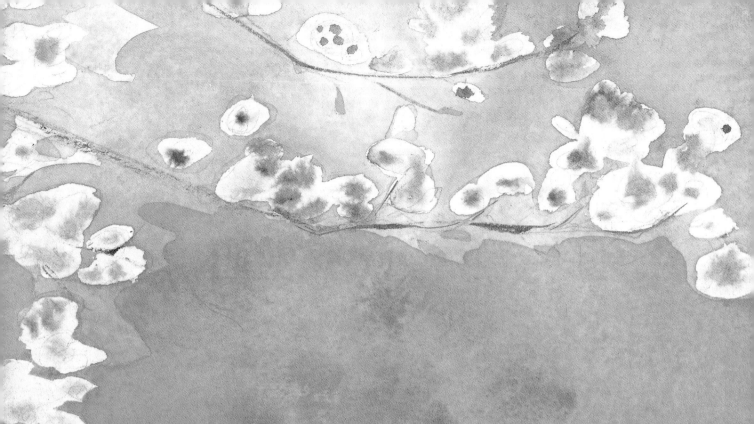

The wait ended on Easter morning. The first photo of the First Dog, a gift from Senator and Mrs. Edward Kennedy, made news. Malia and Sasha plucked a name right from their family tree. Their cousins' cat was named Bo. Also, their late grandfather, Frasier Robinson, was known as Diddley, a nickname borrowed from Chicago bluesman Bo Diddley. So Bo it was. Now the First Lady has a garden helper. The president has a running mate. Malia and Sasha have a new best friend. And pets everywhere have a voice in the White House.

Woof! Woof!

 # About Other White House Pets

President George Washington, a dog breeder, is known as the father of the American fox-hound. He owned more than thirty of the hunting dogs, including one named Drunkard.

President John Quincy Adams kept his pet alligator in the White House.

President Warren G. Harding gave his Airedale terrier, Laddie Boy, a hand-carved chair to sit on during cabinet meetings. At a birthday party that Harding hosted for Laddie Boy, neighborhood dogs feasted on dog-biscuit cake.

President Calvin Coolidge not only had a pair of white collies, but also several more dogs, plus raccoons, canaries, a goose, a mockingbird, a donkey, and a bobcat.

President Herbert Hoover owned a German shepherd named King Tut, two fox terriers named Big Ben and Sonnie, an elkhound named Weejie, and Patrick, an Irish wolfhound—one of the tallest breeds—plus a number of other dogs.

President Franklin D. Roosevelt's Scottish terrier, Fala, was rather famous. The dog starred in a movie, was an honorary U.S. Army private, and had his own press secretary.

President John F. Kennedy was the first commander in chief to ask that his dog meet the presidential helicopter. The Kennedy family owned several dogs, as well as parakeets, ponies, hamsters, a canary, a horse, and a rabbit named Zsa Zsa.

President Lyndon B. Johnson had four beagles and a mixed-breed dog named Yuki that his daughter had found at a gas station. Yuki sang with the president for a British ambassador.

President George H. W. Bush had a springer spaniel named Millie. She had several litters and "authored" a book while in the White House.

President Bill Clinton's pets, Socks the cat and Buddy the chocolate Labrador retriever, did not get along.

President George W. Bush had an English springer spaniel named Spot and two Scottish terriers, Barney and Miss Beazley. Barney had a Web site and occasionally wore a webcam that documented his adventures in the White House.